THE COMIC ADVENTURES OF FELIX THE CAT
© 1983 Felix the Cat Productions, Inc.
From **The Adventures of Felix** comic strip © 1934 King Features Syndicate

Published by DETERMINED PRODUCTIONS, INC.
Box 2150, San Francisco, California 94126

Printed in the United States of America
Library of Congress Card Catalog No. 82-74029
ISBN: 0-915696-62-2

FELIX is not only the world's most famous cat—he's the funniest. Start reading his adventures and you'll find out why.

Millions have been laughing at his antics since the 1920s and some of these people don't even like cats.

THE ARTFUL LODGER

THE COMIC ADVENTURES OF FELIX THE CAT

THE COMIC ADVENTURES OF FELIX THE CAT

THE COMIC ADVENTURES OF FELIX THE CAT

THE COMIC ADVENTURES OF FELIX THE CAT

THE COMIC ADVENTURES OF FELIX THE CAT

SOME PUMPKINS!

THE COMIC ADVENTURES OF FELIX THE CAT

HERE I CAN SNOOZE WITHOUT GETTING THINGS BLAMED ON ME

SO!!

I KNOW YOU DIDN'T DO IT, FELIX — SOMEONE PLANTED THOSE BOTTLES ON YOU SO'S YOU'D BE SUSPECTED OF ALL THE STEALING THAT'S GOING ON — AND TO THROW US OFF HIS TRACK

THAT THIEF CAN'T HIDE ON THIS FARM — I KNOW ALL THE NOOKS

THE COMIC ADVENTURES OF FELIX THE CAT

DE KID IS RIGHT — WE GOT HIM — HOLD HIM IN YOUR TOWN LOCKUP, MEN — I'LL PICK HIM UP LATER FOR THE STATE

FOOLS! DEY DON'T KNOW DAT DEY GOT DE COP AND I GOT HIS UNIFORM — NOW IT'LL BE SAFE FOR ME TO GRAB A REAL FEED IN DE FARM-HOUSE

SHUT UP! WE DON'T WANT NO EXPLANATIONS

SAY, MR. YIMINY — DERE MIGHT BE OTHER PALS OF THAT BANDIT HANGIN' 'ROUND — YA BETTER LET ME PERTECT YOUR MONEY TONIGHT

AS SOON AS DEY FALL ASLEEP I'LL SKIP WIT' DAT SWAG — WON'T DEY KEEL OVER WHEN DEY FIND OUT I'M NO COP, BUT A GEN'LEMEN OF SEIZURE?

THE COMIC ADVENTURES OF FELIX THE CAT

BANDIT LOOT

THE COMIC ADVENTURES OF FELIX THE CAT

THE SCHEMING SCIENTIST

THE COMIC ADVENTURES OF FELIX THE CAT

THAT CAT WOULD LIKE TO GET AWAY, BUT HE'S TOO USEFUL TO ME TO LOSE

I CAN DO A LOT WITH HIM TO FURTHER THE INTEREST OF SCIENCE

THIS MAY NOT BE SUCH A BAD HOME, AFTER ALL, I THINK I'LL STICK AROUND

I'LL TREAT HIM KINDLY FOR A DAY TO WIN HIS CONFIDENCE, THEN I'LL START EXPERIMENTING

THE COMIC ADVENTURES OF FELIX THE CAT

SLEEPLESS NIGHTS

THE COMIC ADVENTURES OF FELIX THE CAT

THE COMIC ADVENTURES OF FELIX THE CAT

THE COMIC ADVENTURES OF FELIX THE CAT

THE COMIC ADVENTURES OF FELIX THE CAT

THE GRAND HOTEL

THE COMIC ADVENTURES OF FELIX THE CAT

THERE'S PLENTY OF EMPTY ROOMS IN THAT HOTEL — WHY SHOULD I WASTE ALL THAT SPACE·?

FINE SO FAR — I GOT BY THE DOORMAN SAFELY

AH! THE CLERK'S ASLEEP — I'LL BORROW ONE OF THE ROOM KEYS

I DREW A LUCKY NUMBER, I HOPE

13

THE COMIC ADVENTURES OF FELIX THE CAT

THE COMIC ADVENTURES OF FELIX THE CAT

FAIR WEATHER FRIENDS

THE COMIC ADVENTURES OF FELIX THE CAT

THAT HOG SURE IS SNOOTY SINCE HE WON THE BLUE RIBBON AT THE COUNTY FAIR

TAKE MY TIP – DON'T EAT ALL THAT HAY – GET YOURSELF IN CONDITION – YOU CAN WIN A BLUE RIBBON, TOO, LIKE THE PIG

YOU'RE RIGHT – I'LL DIET AND GRAB FIRST PRIZE AT THE COUNTY FAIR HORSE SHOW

THAT'S SHOWING HORSE SENSE

THAT GIVES ME A BED FOR TONIGHT ANYWAY

THE COMIC ADVENTURES OF FELIX THE CAT

THE COMIC ADVENTURES OF FELIX THE CAT

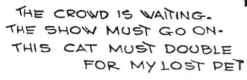

THE COMIC ADVENTURES OF FELIX THE CAT

A CAT - ? ?

I'LL KEEP HIM - A BLACK CAT ALWAYS ADDS A TOUCH OF MYSTERY WHICH WILL IMPRESS MY CLIENTS

I WON'T BE AN ORNAMENT TO SATISFY THE WHIM OF MIND-READER - I CAME HERE FOR EATS.

I KNOW WHAT'S ON THAT CAT'S MIND I'LL LOCK THE ICE-BOX

CLICK

THE COMIC ADVENTURES OF FELIX THE CAT

THE COMIC ADVENTURES OF FELIX THE CAT

THAT CAT SAVED MY SHOW, BUT HOW HE GOT IN THAT HAT, I DON'T KNOW

I'LL KEEP HIM — IT WILL BE A SENSATION TO MAKE HIM DISAPPEAR — LIKE THIS

I'LL FINISH PRACTISING THAT ACT AFTER LUNCH

LET'S SEE NOW — OH, YES — I MAKE THE CAT RE-APPEAR

THE COMIC ADVENTURES OF FELIX THE CAT

THE COMIC ADVENTURES OF FELIX THE CAT

AH, ME! ONCE I WAS HAPPY - THEN CAME THE DAY WHEN THAT CAT CAME AND STOLE MY JOB. NOW I'M DOWN AND OUT

POOR CHAP! HE'S ONLY USED TO LIVING IN A MAGICIAN'S HAT - HE'S NOT USED TO WILD-WOOD WAYS

OMIGOSH!! HUNTING HOUNDS!! THEY'RE ON THAT RABBIT'S TRAIL

SNIFF!

IT'S UP TO ME - I GOT HIM IN THIS PICKLE AND I'LL GET HIM OUT

THE COMIC ADVENTURES OF FELIX THE CAT

YOU FAKER - WE SAW THAT RABBIT JUMP INTO THAT HAT AND WE WANT HIM

YOU'RE HIDING HIM - HURRY UP LET'S SEE WHAT YOU'VE GOT IN THAT HAT

LET'S SEE, HOW DID THE MAGICIAN DO THIS TRICK?

MAYBE THIS IS WHAT YOU MEAN

BONES

THANKS! YOU SAVED MY LIFE

HOP OUT, OLD BOY - THEY'RE GONE

SHADES OF SHERLOCK

THE COMIC ADVENTURES OF FELIX THE CAT

THE COMIC ADVENTURES OF FELIX THE CAT

THE COMIC ADVENTURES OF FELIX THE CAT

THE COMIC ADVENTURES OF FELIX THE CAT

SOMEWHERE, SOMEONE IS BEMOANING THE LOSS OF THIS LOOT — I MUST FIND THE RIGHTFUL OWNER

I'VE LOOKED ALL THROUGH THE "LOST" ADS, BUT SEE NOTHING THAT FITS IN

I'VE GOT IT — I'LL TRACE THE THIEF'S FOOTPRINTS BACKWARD TO THE SCENE OF THE ROBBERY

SHADES OF SHERLOCK! WHY DIDN'T I THINK OF THIS BEFORE?

THE MARAUDING MICE

THE COMIC ADVENTURES OF FELIX THE CAT

THE COMIC ADVENTURES OF FELIX THE CAT

THE COMIC ADVENTURES OF FELIX THE CAT

THE COMIC ADVENTURES OF FELIX THE CAT

THE COMIC ADVENTURES OF FELIX THE CAT

THE COMIC ADVENTURES OF FELIX THE CAT